"Stayed in from recess to read it . . . **CAN'T WAIT FOR NEXT ONE!**"
—Zac A., age 9, Hood River, Ore.

"*Hilo* was **SO GREAT** I couldn't stop reading until I'd finished it. I want to read the next one **NOW**!"
—Jack A., age 10, Brooklyn

"**GINA WAS MY FAVORITE** character because she's into science and soccer like me! I also liked D.J.'s family because it looks like mine!"
—Kiran M., age 7, Carlsbad, Calif.

"*Hilo* is **REALLY, REALLY FUNNY.** It has a **LOT OF LAUGHS.** The raccoon is the funniest."
—Theo M., age 7, Miami, Fla.

"My big brother and I fight over this book. **I CAN'T WAIT** for the second one so we can both read a Hilo book at the same time."
—Nory V., age 8, Montclair, N.J.

"**FANTASTIC. EVERY SINGLE THING ABOUT THIS . . . IS TERRIFIC.**"
—Boingboing.net

"**BETTER THAN THE BEST!**"
—Matteo H-G., age 9, Oakland

"**HIGH ENERGY** and **HILARIOUS**!" —Gene Luen Yang, National Ambassador for Young People's Literature

"**ACTION-PACKED** and **AMAZING FUN.**"
—Brad Meltzer, THE FIFTH ASSASSIN

"*Hilo* is loads of **SLAPSTICK FUN**!"
—Dan Santat, winner of the Caldecott Medal

READ ALL THE HiLo BOOKS!

HILO

BOOK 3

THE GREAT BIG BOOM

BY JUDD WINICK

COLOR BY
STEVE HAMAKER

RANDOM HOUSE 🏠 NEW YORK

Published in the United States by Random House Children's Books,
a division of Penguin Random House LLC, New York.
Random House and the colophon are registered trademarks of Penguin Random House LLC.
Visit us on the Web! randomhousekids.com
Educators and librarians, for a variety of teaching tools, visit us at RHTeachersLibrarians.com
Library of Congress Cataloging-in-Publication Data
Names: Winick, Judd, author, illustrator.
Title: Hilo : the great big boom / by Judd Winick.
Description: First edition. | New York : Random House, [2017] | Series: Hilo ; book 3 | Audience: Ages 8–12. |
Summary: Hilo and DJ, with the help of Polly, the magical warrior cat, travel through a mysterious portal
and battle bad guys, face disgusting food, an angry mom, and powerful magic to save their friend Gina.
Identifiers: LCCN 2016005216 | ISBN 978-0-385-38620-3 (hardcover) |
ISBN 978-0-385-38621-0 (hardcover library binding) | ISBN 978-0-385-38622-7 (ebook)
Subjects: LCSH: Graphic novels. | CYAC: Graphic novels. | Robots—Fiction. |
Extraterrestrial beings—Fiction. | Friendship—Fiction. | Science fiction. |
BISAC: JUVENILE FICTION / Comics & Graphic Novels / Manga. | JUVENILE FICTION /
Action & Adventure / General. | JUVENILE FICTION / Social Issues / Friendship.
Classification: LCC PZ7.7.W57 Hin 2017 | DDC 741.5/973—dc23
MANUFACTURED IN CHINA
10 9 8 7
Book design by John Sazaklis
First Edition
Random House Children's Books supports the First Amendment and celebrates the right to read.

FOR
MOM
AND
DAD

CHAPTER 1

SECRETS

MY NAME IS **DANIEL JACKSON LIM.** BUT EVERYONE CALLS ME **D. J.**

I HAVE TWO BEST FRIENDS.

GINA.

AND **HILO.**

HANG ON!

HILO'S ACTUALLY A **ROBOT** FROM ANOTHER **DIMENSION.**

DON'T ANYBODY BARF!

NO BARFING!

GO FASTER!

GOING FASTER!

HE'S GOT A SECRET **LAB** IN HIS BASEMENT.

HOW BIG **IS** THIS PLACE?

A FEW MILES.

MANGOES

WHO WANTS MANGOES?

2

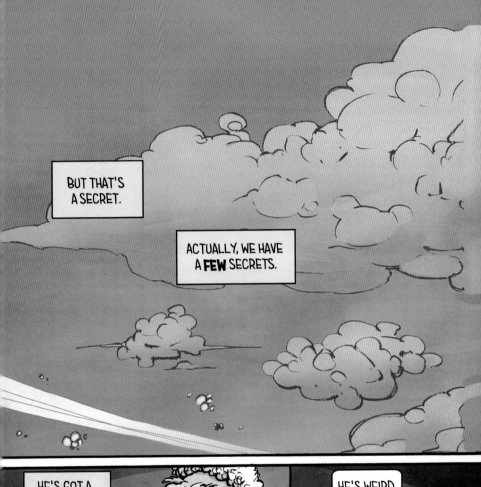

BUT THAT'S A SECRET.

ACTUALLY, WE HAVE A **FEW** SECRETS.

HE'S GOT A **ROBOT** HE BUILT THAT HE PRETENDS IS HIS **UNCLE TROUT.**

I'VE GOT BARBECUING TO DO!

HE'S WEIRD.

YEP.

MANGO?

3

DOGS REALLY LIKE HIM. **A LOT.** (THAT'S NOT REALLY A SECRET, BUT IT'S WEIRD.)

WHAT'S UP, FURRY FELLAS?!

AND THERE ARE HUGE SECRETS. LIKE **RAZORWARK,** AN EVIL ROBOT WHO'S AT WAR WITH ALL THE HUMANS ON HILO'S WORLD.

HE SENT AN ARMY OF **VEGETABLES** TO DESTROY EARTH.

HILO STOPPED THE

BUT GINA...

GINA, WHO IS THE **SMARTEST** OF US.

THE **BRAVEST.**

MY BEST FRIEND.

DON'T LET GO!

4

NO!

D.J.!

GINA GOT SUCKED INTO A PORTAL....

WE DON'T KNOW WHERE SHE IS.

WE'LL GET HER BACK.

BUT I GUESS WHEN HILO SAVED THE WORLD FROM THE EVIL VEGETABLES, WE DIDN'T DO TOO GOOD A JOB KEEPING IT A **SECRET**.

YEP. I WAS RIGHT! THEY **DO!**

YEAH!

BUT I **CAN'T** GO WITH **THEM.**

NO!

WE HAVE TO RESCUE GINA.

YEAH.

WE CAN'T BE TAKEN PRISONER BY THE ARMY **AND** GO GET GINA, RIGHT?

RIGHT!

SERGEANT! RESTRAIN THE PRISONERS!

YES SIR!

PLACE YOUR HANDS BEHIND YOUR HEAD!

HILO, WE'VE GOT TO GET AWAY.

YES.

BUT I'M NOT HURTING ANYONE.

9

REEEEP

HUUUUUCK

OUTSTANDING.

OH! OH! EW! NASTY!

YOU MADE MY TUMMY GO YUCKY! WAAAH!

WAAAH!

SIR, ONE OF THEM IS **PUKING.**

I CAN SEE THAT TOO!

I THINK I CAN GO AGAIN.

FIRE AWAY, SOLDIER.

HUUUUUCK.

REPEAT BUSINESS.

THESE BOYS ARE A THREAT TO NATIONAL SECURITY?

WELL, **THIS** ONE SHOOTS LASERS FROM HIS HANDS.

I NEED TO GO PEE.

ME TOO.

I WANT HEADQUARTERS ON THE PHONE. **NOW.**

AND FIND 'EM SOME-PLACE THEY CAN TINKLE.

AND DO YOU HAVE ANY MANGOES?

AOOOOooO OOoooo

CHAPTER 2

HELP

SECTOR 8 HOLDING CELL.

BUT NO MANGOES. AND THESE COOKIES THEY GAVE US ARE THE WORST. **BLECH.** COCONUT.

HILO. **FOCUS.**

I MEAN, AT SOME POINT REAL SOON, THEY'RE GOING TO FIGURE OUT THAT YOU **ARE** THAT BOY WHO WAS FLYING AROUND SHOOTING LASERS FROM YOUR HANDS -- AND THEY'RE **NOT** GOING TO LET YOU LEAVE!

AND WE NEED TO GO GET **GINA!**

I THOUGHT YOU WEREN'T GOING TO LET THEM CAPTURE US.

WHY? I NEED THEIR HELP.

HELP?

WELL, NOT REALLY **HELP.** BUT I NEED THEIR STUFF.

15

16

WE ZIP THROUGH THE PORTAL. YOU **AND** ME. I'M COMING WITH YOU.

IT COULD BE... DANGEROUS.

OKAY.

HILO... AFTER GINA GOT PULLED INTO THE PORTAL, YOU SAID THAT YOU STARTED TO REMEMBER YOUR **PAST.**

YOU SAID YOU USED TO BE... **BAD.**

THAT YOU DID **TERRIBLE** THINGS ON YOUR WORLD.

YOU...YOU **HELPED** RAZORWARK?

YES.

THAT'S WHAT I REMEMBER.

YOU DESTROYED CITIES?

YES.

YOU...YOU **KILLED** PEOPLE?

NO! THE CITIES WERE **EMPTY!** THAT...

BUT... YOU **CHANGED.** YOU TURNED ON HIM. YOU TRIED TO STOP HIM.

YOU **FOUGHT** HIM.

YES.

I CHANGED.

WHY?

I DON'T REMEMBER.

WHAT'S IN HERE?

IT SAYS THEY'RE CALLED **THE ORBS OF FELLBECK.**

SHUCK

SHUC

ZAP

ZAP

ZAP

BOOM BOOM BOOM

IT SAYS THAT EACH ORB CAN ERASE THE **MEMORIES** OF AN ENTIRE WORLD FROM **TWO SUNSETS.**

TWO SUNSETS? DOES THAT MEAN **EVERYONE** ON EARTH WILL FORGET THE LAST **TWO DAYS?**

EXCEPT THE ONES **HOLDING** THE ORBS AND DOING THE SPELL.

SO NOBODY BUT **US** WILL REMEMBER THE RAPSCALLIONS, PORTALS, MONSTERS --

OR A FLYING KID SHOOTING **LASERS!**

WHAT DO WE DO?!

24

AAAAAAH!

SLOW DOWN!

CAN'T! WE MIGHT NOT MAKE IT!

THE PORTAL THAT GETS US TO GINA IS ONLY OPEN A LITTLE WHILE LONGER!

HILO?!

WE'RE FLYING INTO A MOUNTAIN!

AAAAAH!!

HIIIIIIIIIIIILOOOOOOOO!!

33

PLEASE DON'T TELL ME YOU RAN OUT OF POWER AND YOU'RE ASLEEP.

Z Z Z Z
Z Z Z

HEH.

WANT A COCONUT COOKIE?

RoOoOoOoAR

37

39

AAAH! WORSE TIME TO NAP! ANGRY TALKING ALLIGATOR SHOOTING LASERS!

TZOT

I MADE YOU DIFFERENTLY FROM THEM.

44

I DON'T KNOW WHAT'S WORSE ABOUT YOU HAIRLESS MONKEYS-- HOW BAD YOU **SMELL** ...

OR THAT YOU'RE ALWAYS GETTING LOST.

POLLY!

HAZZAH.

47

HI, GUYS.

GINA?

YEAH. I --

HI.

HI.

ARE YOU OKAY? YOU **LOOK** OKAY? BUT I MEAN, **ARE** YOU OKAY?

I'M OKAY.

49

I THINK HE'S HAPPY TO SEE HER.

I THINK SO TOO.

HI, GINA!

HI, HILO. SO YOU FOUND A PORTAL.

YEAH. BUT WE HAD TO GET CAPTURED BY THE ARMY FIRST.

THE ARMY?

LONG STORY.

AND THE ARMY HAS TERRIBLE COOKIES.

REALLY?

YEAH.

WHAT'S A COOKIE?

I LIKE YOUR OUTFIT, GINA. ALL BOOTY-KICKING-WARRIOR-LOOKING STUFF.

THANKS. POLLY GAVE IT TO ME. MY CLOTHES GOT DIRTY AFTER A FEW DAYS.

DAYS? WHAT DO YOU MEAN **DAYS?** YOU GOT SUCKED INTO THAT PORTAL A FEW HOURS AGO.

D.J., I'VE BEEN HERE FOR **THREE MONTHS.**

WHAT?!

AYE. "PORTALS." WE CALL 'EM DOORS. AND THEY ARE ALWAYS A SLIPPERY SPOT O'BUSINESS. YOU BOYS MUST'VE HOPPED THROUGH ONE THAT TOSSED YOU INTO THE FUTURE A WEE BIT.

OOPS.

WELL, WE'RE GETTING OUT OF HERE. NOW, HILO, WHERE DO WE FIND A PORTAL TO HOME?

SORRY?

HOME. WE'VE GOT GINA, AND NOW WE CAN GO TO EARTH.

OH.

I DON'T KNOW. I HAVEN'T ACTUALLY FIGURED OUT HOW TO GET US BACK.

WHAT? WHAT DO YOU **MEAN** -- HOW COULD YOU NOT KNOW HOW TO GET US BACK?!

WELL, THERE WAS **A LOT** GOING ON. THERE WAS THE ARMY. THERE WERE THE TERRIBLE COOKIES. AND I WAS REALLY FOCUSED ON GETTING GINA.

WHICH HE DID.

WHICH I DID.

YEAH! THREE MONTHS INTO THE FUTURE WITH NO WAY HOME?!

TRUE. I KIND OF BLEW IT THERE.

KIND OF?!

OKAY, D.J. IS HAVING A WEE BIT OF A **NUTTY.** AND I LIKE A GOOD NUTTY, BUT WE NEED TO BE ON OUR WAY BEFORE WE'RE UP TO OUR ARMPITS IN LIZARDS.

WHAT?

KIND OF?!

AYE, WE NEED TO BE OFF. THAT PUTRID, SLIME-CAKED SALAMANDER RIDING THE GIANT BALL OF HAIR IS PART OF THE **SCALE TAIL CLAN.**

THE SCALE TAIL CLAN USE WIRE, IRON, AND LIGHTNING.

MACHINES.

THAT ONE THAT GOT AWAY WILL BE BACK WITH HIS MATES, AND **SOON.**

AND EVEN THOUGH I'M IN DISGUISE, THEY MIGHT RECOGNIZE ME AS A MEMBER OF THE **FURBACK CLAN,** SO WE SHOULD BE **VERY** FAR FROM HERE WHEN THEY RETURN.

I GUESS YOUR CLANS DON'T GET ALONG VERY WELL.

NO. NOT VERY WELL.

THEY'VE BEEN TRYING TO CONQUER US FOR FIVE HUNDRED YEARS.

CHAPTER

FUR
AND SCALE

THE VILLAGE OF THE **SCALE TAIL CLAN.**

BUT, **GREAT BOOMBA,** THE SMALL HOODED ONE WAS POWERFUL.

MAKE MORE.

HOOOOOM

FIRE ORB NOT GIVE YOU WHAT YOU WANT, GREAT BOOMBA?

THE FIRE ORB GIVE ME WHATEVER I ASK.

IT GIVES **EVERY** BOOMBA BEFORE ME FOR FIVE HUNDRED YEARS! IT MAKE WHAT SCALE TAIL CLAN NEED...

OR IT SUFFERS.

GOOD.

CLANG

GREAT BOOMBA, BEFORE HOODED ONE CAME AND MADE MAGIC, I CHASE TWO MONKEYS WITH NO FUR.

MAKE FIFTY OF THIS.

SHUNK

ONE MONKEY, IT FLEW. AND SHOOT THE **FIRE** FROM HANDS.

IT MAGIC?

NO! THE FIRE FROM HANDS, MORE LIKE SCALE TAIL **WEAPON** FIRE.

MACHINE FIRE. WHAT FLYING MONKEY LOOK LIKE?

YELLOW HAIR ON HEAD. RED CLOTH ON BACK. THIS ON CHEST.

SCRRRR

SCRAAAAAATCH

60

I NOT KNOW THIS MARK.

BOOooooooo

WHAT'S WRONG WITH FIRE ORB?

POONT

CHUNK

THAT IS HIM.

THAT IS YELLOW-HAIRED MONKEY. HE SHOOT MACHINE FIRE.

IN THE DESERT OF THE FOLDED EEL.

BUT AS THE STORIES GO, FIVE CENTURIES AGO, THE SCALE TAIL CLAN USED TO BE A GAGGLE OF THIEVING, DIRT-SCRATCHING TUNKER HEADS, **BARELY** ABLE TO SURVIVE.

AND THEY WERE **DUMB!** AS DUMB AS A PILE OF HAMMERS! WAIT -- **NO! DUMBER!** IF THE SCALE TAILS STUDIED **ALL** DAY AND **ALL** NIGHT, THEY **STILL** WOULDN'T BE WITHIN SPITTING DISTANCE OF THE STUPIDITY OF A PILE OF HAMMERS!

WHAT WE EAT? IT TASTE TERRIBLE.

IT ROCKS.

64

METAL THAT SHOOTS **FIRE.** METAL SHIPS THAT **CARRY THEM.** METAL **SKINS.** METAL THAT **EXPLODES.**

THEY DIDN'T NEED MAGIC, AND THEY CONQUERED **ALL** OF OSHUN. THEY RULE OUR ENTIRE WORLD.

THEY EVEN RULE THE FURBACK CLAN?

ARE YOU **DAFT,** LASER MITTS? YOU THINK **OUR** MIGHTY CLAN WOULD LIE DOWN TO **THOSE** FORK-TONGUED WOBBYNAPS?!

NEVER!

WE ARE FURBACK CLAN!

THIS IS **AMAZING.**

WELL, AFTER A FEW MONTHS...

IT'S **STILL** AMAZING!

HEY!

AAAH!

WHAT ARE YOU DOING? WERE YOU TRYING TO **PET** ME?

I DIDN'T KNOW YOU COULD TALK.

SO? THAT MEANS YOU CAN PET ME?

SORRY, HE'S NEW.

NO KIDDING.

DON'T MIND HIM, D. J.

AAAH!

YOU'LL FIND THAT THE FURBACK CLAN ARE THE MOST FRIENDLY AND WELCOMING CREATURES ON **THIS** OR ANY WORLD.

OH! I AM GOING TO CHUCK A WOBBLY!!

WITH SOME SMALL EXCEPTIONS.

POLLANDRA PACK WALLACE BRIMDALE KORIMAKO! ARE YOU **DAFT?!** HAVE YOUR BRAINS **ESCAPED** YOUR MELON?!

I'D SAY YOU'VE TAKEN LEAVE OF YOUR SENSES, BUT THAT WOULD IMPLY YOU **HAVE** SENSES!

WHAT ARE YOU BREAKING STICKS ABOUT?

I AM ENJOYING THIS **SO** MUCH.

OH! **HEY!**

WHAT'S UP, FELLAS?!

HI.

HELLO.

HEY.

HOW'S IT GOIN'?

CUTE.

I'M GUESSING YOU'LL BE WANTING TO GET BACK TO BERT.

THEY'LL NEED A DOOR.

THEY'LL NEED THE IMMENSE POWER OF THE EXALTED HIGH LORD **NECROMANCER.** HE CAN HELP WITH THAT.

WELL, WE DON'T WANT TO BOTHER ANY OF THE IMMENSE-POWER GUYS.

IT'S OKAY.

HE'S MY DAD.

MOST NEVER STAY OPEN FOR LONG, AND THEN THEY SHUT FOR **YEARS.** AS YOU ALREADY LEARNED, A DOOR MAY EVEN POP YOU **FORWARD** OR **BACK** IN TIME.

SO SEARCHING FOR THE **RIGHT** DOOR IS CAREFUL AND DELICATE WORK. IT REQUIRES **CONCENTRATION** AND **DEEP STUDY.**

A **QUIET** MIND IS ONE THAT FINDS THE UNSEEN PATH.

77

CRASH

LADS! I'M TRYING TO HAVE A BIT OF A THINK OVER HERE!

SORRY, DA!

MUM! CANDICE TOOK MY LEVITATION CLOAK!

SHE'S NOT SUPPOSED TO BE LEVITATING UNTIL SHE'S PASSED HER EXAM!

HOW CAN I **PASS** IF I DON'T **PRACTICE,** YA GIT?!

GRRR RRRR

CRASH

DO IT AGAIN!

SETTLE DOWN, YA BAGS OF HAIR, OR I'LL HAVE YA SLEEPING OUTSIDE!

SORRY, MUM!

ARE THEY ALWAYS LIKE THIS?

NO, USUALLY THEY'RE PRETTY LOUD.

THIS FOOD IS KIND OF BAD.

OH, YOU DON'T HAVE TO WHISPER. THEY KNOW IT'S DISGUSTING, BUT THEY EAT IT ANYWAY.

BECAUSE WE ARE FURBACK CLAN!!

HEH. I KNOW. I --

AAAH! GIANT BUG!

OH, THAT'S OUR COCKROACH, RHEMUS.

WHO'S A GOOD BOY? **YOU** ARE. YES, YOU ARE.

HILO, I THINK I CAN HELP YOU RASCALS.

YOU CAN?

AYE. SINCE WE'VE GOT **THREE** OF YOU HERE FROM PLANET **BERT**...

EARTH.

AYE. I CAN LOCATE IT. YOU ALL **STINK** WITH **VAPOR** OF THAT WORLD.

PORTAL JUICE!

"PORTAL JUICE"? WELL, DIFFERENT NAME, SAME **STUFF**. WHAT YOUR WORLD CALLS **SCIENCE**, WE CALL **MAGIC**.

HEY! I WAS EATING THAT!

YEAH! YOU **WERE**.

OOH. THERE SHE IS.

A PERFECTLY FINE DOOR THAT WILL OPEN THIRTY MILES AWAY. RIGHT THROUGH **THE UNCANNY VALLEY.**

BUT IT'LL JUST BE OPEN FOR A WEE BIT.

THAT'LL TAKE A DAY AND A HALF BY PAW.

I COULD FLY US THERE REAL QUICK.

NO. NO FLYING. YOU MAY BE SEEN. THE SCALE TAILS HAVE GOT EYES IN THE SKIES. METAL BIRDS AND BATS WHO TELL THEIR MASTERS EVERYTHING. NAY, YOU'LL NEED TO HOOF IT UNDER THE COVER OF HILLS AND TREES.

84

CONNOR.

DA... THAT'S DANGEROUS.

I WASN'T AWARE THAT WE **KORIMAKOS** TURNED AWAY FROM DANGER.

THE BOY'S NOT A KORIMAKO.

AND I'M NOT A **BOY.** I'M A MACHINE. I'M NOT ALIVE. I DON'T THINK YOUR MAGICAL SPELLS WOULD WORK ON ME.

I'M NOT A MAN. I'M A **CAT**.

AND YOU ... YOU ARE JUST ANOTHER LIVING BEING.

YOU **THINK**. YOU **FEEL**.

ONE WORLD'S MAGIC IS JUST ANOTHER WORLD'S SCIENCE.

LET HIM TRY.

OKAY.

DEEP IN THE SEA, BELOW THE MURK.
BENEATH THE CAVERNS, TRAPPED IN THE DIRT.
RISE UP FROM THE GROUND, OVERTURN THE DARK MOSS ...

RETURN TO US THE VISIONS **WE HAVE LOST!**

WHUMP

HILO!

HILO, YOUR MEMORIES ARE TOO WELL BURIED.

THERE'S SOME MIGHTY POWERFUL MAGIC AT WORK HERE THAT'S TRYING TO **KEEP** YOU FROM REMEMBERING. YOU NEED A MORE POWERFUL **SPELL WIELDER** THAN ME.

WHO'S BETTER THAN YOU, DA?

HILO NEEDS **LADY SKYLARK.**

AYE.

THAT'S ALL FINE AND GOOD, BUT HOW ARE **THESE** THREE GOING TO FIND HER?

I'LL TAKE THEM.

WHAT NOW?! LADY SKYLARK IS **MILES** OUTSIDE THE SAFE ZONE.

SHE'S JUST OFF THE EDGE OF **THE UNCANNY VALLEY.**

RIGHT WHERE D.J., GINA, AND HILO'S DOOR BACK TO BERT WILL OPEN. IT'S ON THE WAY.

CAN I GO TOO, MUM?!

OI!

IF CAROLINE IS GOIN', THEN **I'M** GOIN'!

IF CAROLINE AND MOIRA ARE GOING, THEN **I'M** GOING TOO!

ME TOO!

98

NO ONE IS GOING!

THE **FURBACK CLAN** HAS BEEN SAFELY HIDDEN FOR **CENTURIES.**

GIT.

WOLLY BACK.

NAPPER.

POLLY, IF A SCALE TAIL GETS AHOLD OF YA, YOU MAY BE **WORSE** THAN **KILLED.**

THEY MAY **HURT** YOU UNTIL YOU TELL THEM WHERE OUR VILLAGE IS.

THEN I BEST NOT GET CAUGHT.

NO.

YOU'RE NOT GOING.

I'VE PUT YOU ALL IN ENOUGH DANGER. I GOT GINA PULLED TO THIS WORLD. I ALMOST BLEW UP YOUR HOUSE.

IT'S NOT WORTH IT.

WE SHOULD JUST GO BACK TO EARTH.

NO. WE NEED TO FIND OUT ABOUT YOUR **PAST.**

RAZORWARK SAID HE WAS COMING BACK, RIGHT?

YES.

IF YOU'RE GOING TO BEAT HIM... IF **WE'RE** GOING TO BEAT HIM... WE NEED TO KNOW EVERYTHING.

YOU ASKED ME TO BE BRAVE. SO, I'M BEING BRAVE.

THIS LADY SKYLARK WILL HELP HIM?

AYE.

THAT'S WHERE WE HAVE TO GO.

MUM, WE CAN'T HIDE FOREVER. WE NEED TO BE BRAVE TOO.

YOU'RE RIGHT... IF IT'S WHAT HILO REALLY NEEDS.

OKAY.

LET'S GO.

BROKEN

NO TRAIL. NO FOOTPRINTS.

HOODED ONE WAS USING MAGIC. MUST HAVE DONE SPELL TO NOT LEAVE TRACKS.

THEN HOW WE FIND YELLOW-HAIRED APE?

WITH THIS.

WHAT THAT?

FINDER MACHINE.

BEEP

BEEP BEEP

THERE ... IT SAYS THEY GO THAT WAY.

BEEP BEEP BEEP BEEP BEEP

FIRE ORB NEVER MAKE FINDER MACHINE BEFORE. WHY IT MAKE NOW?

NOT KNOW.

BEEP BEE BEE BE

BUT GREAT BOOMBA **WANT** YELLOW-HAIRED APE.

BEEP BEE BE

SO, WE **GET** YELLOW-HAIRED APE.

I AM HUNGRY.

ME TOO.

WANT TO EAT ROCKS?

YES.

ON THE KLIBAN RIVER.

WHY DID THE GIRL GIVE HER PONY **COUGH SYRUP?**

WHY?

BECAUSE HE WAS A **LITTLE HORSE!**

HA HA HA HA HA HA

LISTEN, LISTEN, LISTEN --

WHERE DO GENERALS KEEP THEIR **ARMIES?**

WHERE?

IN THEIR **SLEEVIES.**

HA HA HA HA HA **HA!**

LISTEN! LISTEN! THERE'S TWO MUFFINS IN AN OVEN!

ONE MUFFIN TURNS TO THE **OTHER** MUFFIN AND SAYS, "BOY, IT'S **HOT** IN HERE."

THE OTHER MUFFIN SAYS, **"HOLY MACKEREL! A TALKING MUFFIN!"**

AAAAH HA HA HA HA HA HA HA HA HÁA.AA

WHAT'S A MUFFIN?

WHY DO DUCKS HAVE FLAT FEET?

WHY?

TO STAMP OUT FOREST FIRES.

WHAT?

BLUB

WAIT! WHY DO ELEPHANTS HAVE FLAT FEET?

WHY?

TO STAMP OUT FLAMING DUCKS!

AAAAH HA HA HA! BECAUSE THE DUCKS ARE ON FIRE!

YEAH!

HA! DUCKS ARE SO STUPID!

YEAAAAH! NOT SO TOUGH **NOW**, ARE YA? I SHOULD PUT YA ON THE END OF A FISHING POLE AND USE YA AS **BAIT**, YA WEE SPITTER!

HO-HOOO, GINA! DID YOU **SEE** OUR WEE SORCERESS AT WORK?!

SHE CAN **ALREADY** DO A SUMMONING SPELL TO FIRE UP SOME WANDS, AND A STOPPER HEX THAT'LL KNOCK FIVE TONS OF TENTACLES ON ITS **BUTT!**

YEAH! THAT WAS A BIG PILE OF --

OUT! **STAND!** **ING!**

WHAT ELSE CAN YOU DO? CAN YOU MAKE ME TALLER? OH, OH, OH -- OR SUMMON SOME MANGOES? **THAT** WOULD BE MAGICAL!

NO, I --

WHUMP

WHAT IS WRONG WITH YOU?!

WHAT?

I SAID -- WHAT IS **WRONG** WITH YOU?!

ME? D.J., I --

NOT **YOU.**

HIM.

POLLY COULD HAVE BEEN **KILLED.** YOU JUST WATCHED THAT **THING** GRAB HER!

YOU DIDN'T DO ANYTHING!

GINA STOPPED IT.

YEAH! BECAUSE **YOU** DIDN'T!

AND THIS WASN'T THE FIRST TIME! WHEN THE ALLIGATOR WAS CHASING US IN THE DESERT-- YOU DIDN'T DO ANYTHING EITHER!

AND YOU DIDN'T WANT TO GO TO LADY SKYLARK'S TO GET YOUR MEMORIES BACK, DID YOU?

EVERYONE IS DOING **EVERYTHING** THEY CAN TO HELP YOU --

EXCEPT YOU!

WHY?!

WHAT IN THE BLUDNDJ?

WHAT?!

WHAT IF I'M BROKEN?!

WHAT DO YOU MEAN?

EVERY TIME I USE MY POWERS, I FEEL LIKE I'M GETTING STRONGER. AND THE STRONGER I GET...

I FEEL LIKE I'M CLOSER TO REMEMBERING EVERYTHING.

ISN'T THAT WHAT WE WANT?

WHAT IF I'M BAD?

WHAT IF I'M REALLY JUST A **WEAPON** THAT **RAZORWARK** MADE?

MAYBE BEING **GOOD** IS HOW I AM **ONLY** WHEN I'M BROKE N...

IF I LET MYSELF BE AS POWERFUL AS I CAN BE...

WHAT IF I'M **FIXED**...

AND I'M **EVIL?**

WHAT IF I'M JUST A **BAD MACHINE.**

119

YOU'RE **NOT.**

YOU DON'T KNOW THAT.

I TOLD YOU. I DON'T KNOW WHY I STARTED BEING GOOD.

WHAT IF I'M JUST...

BROKEN?

THE SUNS ARE GOING DOWN. WE OUGHT TO GET SOME SLEEP.

MY MUM ALWAYS SAYS, "EVERYTHING IS BRIGHTER IN THE MORNING."

Z Zz zzZZz
I'LL TWIST YER
TENTACLES INTO
KNOTS AND WEAR
YOU AS A HAT...
SNORT...

ZZ
ZZZ

YOU HAVING TROUBLE SLEEPING?

SORT OF.

THE SUNS ARE STRONGER, AND THE ATMOSPHERE IS CLEANER THAN ON EARTH. MY POWER CELLS ARE FULL.

I CAN'T SHUT DOWN.

I DIDN'T KNOW YOU RAN ON SOLAR ENERGY.

I DIDN'T EITHER. I REMEMBERED YESTERDAY.

Y'KNOW, I'VE BEEN READING ABOUT THE HISTORY OF **OSHUN.**

YEAH?

THREE MONTHS WITH NO TV OR BOOKS, AND THESE ANCIENT SCROLLS THEY HAVE START TO LOOK PRETTY GOOD.

DID YOU KNOW **EVERYONE** ON OSHUN USED TO BE AT WAR WITH ONE ANOTHER?

IT WAS AWFUL.

I WAS READING ABOUT THIS GUY... **TAMIR.** OVER TWO THOUSAND YEARS AGO, HE WAS THE ONE WHO UNITED ALL THE DIFFERENT TRIBES AND CLANS.

SO, HE WAS A GREAT LEADER.

FROM WHAT I READ? HE WAS ... **A MONSTER.** HE CAUSED MOST OF THE WARS.

REALLY?

YEAH. HE SPENT YEARS AND YEARS CONQUERING AND DESTROYING. HE WAS LIKE THIS UNENDING STORM OF GREED AND RAGE.

VILLAGES WOULD HANG HIS FLAG AT THEIR HIGHEST PEAKS **BEFORE** HE COULD INVADE, JUST SO HE COULD SEE THAT THEY **WANTED** TO SURRENDER AND HE DIDN'T HAVE TO ATTACK THEM.

BUT TAMIR WOULD ATTACK THEM ANYWAY.

THEN, WHEN PEOPLE FEARED HIM MORE THAN ANYTHING, WHEN HE'D TORN HIS WAY ACROSS THE ENTIRE PLANET AND ALL OF OSHUN WAS UNDER HIS CONTROL...

HE STOPPED.

STOPPED?

YEP. HE SENT HIS ARMY AWAY. FREED EVERYONE HE'D CONQUERED. SWORE HE'D NEVER HURT ANOTHER LIVING THING AS LONG AS HE LIVED.

AND HE BURIED HIS SWORD IN THE GROUND.

TAMIR SPENT THE NEXT HUNDRED YEARS WRITING, TEACHING, AND LIVING IN PEACE. THE WORLD LISTENED TO HIM. AND FOR OVER A THOUSAND YEARS, OSHUN WAS A WORLD WITHOUT WAR.

WHAT HAPPENED? WHY DID HE STOP? WHY ... WHY DID HE CHANGE?

NO ONE KNOWS.

EXCEPT TAMIR.

CHAPTER 7

THE GREAT BIG BOOM

128

ONE RIDE INSIDE A GIANT FISH LATER . . .

CACK

IF I WERE TO TRY TO PULL THE MEMORIES TO THE SURFACE, IT WOULD **KILL** THIS APE.

HIS BODY IS JUST MEAT AND BONE AND BLOOD. MY SPELLS WOULD TEAR HIM APART.

I'M NOT MEAT AND BONE AND BLOOD.

WHAT?

I'M NOT MEAT AND BONE AND BLOOD. I'M A MACHINE.

HOOOOM

137

AND NO ONE CAN HEAR OR SEE US.

HILO.

THAT'S ME.

WHEN ALL THE AIR **BOOMS** OUT OF YOU. **THE GREAT BIG BOOM!**

LAUGHING? YOU MEAN **LAUGHING.**

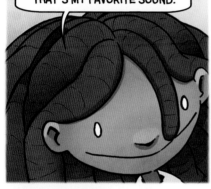

YES. I LIKE IT WHEN YOU DO IT. THAT'S MY FAVORITE SOUND.

WHAM

142

144

SHE WILL BE DEACTIVATED.

WHOA! IT FEELS LIKE SOMETHING CRASHED INTO THE BUILDING.

NO...

WE'RE IN HILO'S **HEAD.** WE SHOULDN'T FEEL **ANYTHING.**

YEAH. THAT'S NOT HAPPENING **HERE.** THAT'S HAPPENING BACK AT MY **HOUSE.**

YOU KNOW, WHERE OUR **BODIES** ARE.

ISN'T THAT YOUR FISH?

YEP.

AAAAAAAA AAAAAAAH!!

HOLY MACKEREL.

CHAPTER 8

BETTER THAN APE

THEY GOT HERE QUICKER THAN I THOUGHT THEY WOULD.

YOU KNEW THE SCALE TAILS WERE COMING?

YES. I FIGURED THEY'D BE CHASING YOUR FRIEND. THOSE REPTILES **LIVE** FOR MACHINES. AND A LIVING MACHINE IS SOMETHING THEY'D **REALLY** WANT.

AND HISTORY ALWAYS REPEATS ITSELF.

WHAT?

NO TIME FOR TALK! WE'RE GOING BACK.

150

UH-OH.

WHY "UH-OH"?

HE WON'T LET GO.

HE'S NOT LETTING US GO BACK.

HILO'S HANGING ON TO THIS MEMORY.

LOOK! INSIDE! FINDER SAY YELLOW-HAIRED APE INSIDE!

GO!

BEEP BEEP BEEP BEEP

WHUMP

WHUMP

WHUMP

BRUMBLE

BRUMBLE

IF WE'RE ASLEEP, WE CAN'T PROTECT OURSELVES!!

HILO! LET US GO BACK!

THE **HOUSE** WILL BUY US SOME TIME.

WHAT?!

MY HOUSE!

IT'S GOT **SKILLS!**

YELLOW-HAIRED APE.

COOM

GRRRRR...

YELLOW-HAIRED APE MAKE **SHIELD.**

WAIT. WHO THAT?

FURBACK CLAN.

MY HOUSE IS ALMOST OUT OF TRICKS! WE NEED TO **GO!**

NOT YET! CAN YOU FEEL IT?!

FEEL **WHAT?!**

HE'S REMEMBERING SOMETHING BIG!

BUT WE--

OI.

I FEEL... I FEEL LIKE I'M...

FLOATING.

POLLY!

158

159

THE **SCALE TAIL CLAN** TOOK POLLY!

IT'S OKAY.

IT'S **NOT** OKAY!

IT IS.

I PROMISE.

I REMEMBER.

CHAPTER

GOOD

VILLAGE OF THE SCALE TAIL CLAN.

WHERE IS **FURBACK CLAN** VILLAGE?

I NOT HURT YOU IF YOU TELL ME.

AND I NOT HURT FURBACK CLAN. JUST WANT FURBACK CLAN TO **JOIN** SCALE TAIL.

THEN ... **EVERYONE** ON OSHUN IS SCALE TAIL.

EVERYBODY HAPPY.

TELL ME.

WHAT YOU SAY?

I SAID:
GET STUFFED, SNAKE FACE!
PFFFFFT!

GRRRRR

FIRE ORB! MAKE MACHINE TO PUNISH THIS HAIRY THING!

TUNG

WOW.

SO, **THIS** IS THE VILLAGE OF THE SCALE TAIL CLAN. I **GOTTA** TELL YOU --

THIS JOINT IS **UGLY.**

HAVE YOU EVER THOUGHT ABOUT PLANTING SOME GRASS? I JUST ATE SOME THAT TASTED LIKE PINEAPPLE. OUTSTANDING! IT MIGHT PEP UP THE PLACE.

DESTROY YELLOW-HAIRED APE.

Y'KNOW, WITH ALL THESE WEAPONS, YOU GUYS MIGHT HAVE BEEN ABLE TO HURT ME.

BUT THAT WAS **BEFORE.**

BEFORE WHAT?

BEFORE I REMEMBERED THE MANY, MANY, **MANY** THINGS I CAN DO.

NO. THAT WAS AN **ELECTROMAGNETIC PULSE.** IT'S A SHORT BURST OF ENERGY THAT'S GENERALLY DISRUPTIVE OR DAMAGING TO ELECTRONIC EQUIPMENT.

I CAN DO THAT.

SO, **YEAH!** "WEAPONS NOT WORK."

OR YOUR FLYING SHIPS. OR YOUR BOMBS.

WE STILL DESTROY YOU.

THERE IS THOUSANDS OF US. YOU ARE ALONE.

OH, NOT REALLY. I INVITED A FEW FRIENDS TO THIS PARTY. MAYBE WE CAN PUT SOME SNACKS OUT FOR THEM. BUT I'D GUESS WHAT YOU GUYS EAT IS PRETTY GROSS. STILL, THEY'LL EAT IT ANYWAY.

YOU KNOW WHY?

MAKE! MORE!

GRRRRRRR

CRACK

EEEEEEEEEE EEE

MAKE MORE OR I HURT MORE!

UH-OH.

CRASH

POLLY.

GOTCHA.

SOMEONE WANTED TO SAY **HI.**

WHEP

HEY, MUM.

HELLO, SWEET-HEART.

THANKS FOR COMING TO GET ME.

WELL, I HAD TO BE BRAVE, DIDN'T I?

'SIDES, WHO'S GONNA HELP ME CLEAN UP THIS MESS?

HAZZAH!

OI! HILO!

YOU'VE GOT TO GET TO THAT TOWER!

177

WHAT **ARE** YOU DOING? THIS THING HAS BEEN MAKING YOUR WEAPONS FOR CENTURIES AND NOW YOU'RE **HITTING** IT?

THAT'S NOT VERY NICE! I'M --

WHAT... WHAT HAPPENED?

HOOM

OI! D.J.! GINA!

Hoooo

FIND HILO AND GET TO THAT DOOR TO EARTH! IT CLOSES SOON --

AND THERE WON'T BE ANOTHER ONE FOR **HUNDREDS** OF YEARS!

YOU KNOW WHERE WE NEED TO GO, RIGHT? WE NEED TO FLY FAST. HELP ME FLY REALLY, REALLY FAST. OKAY?

FROM **MY** WORLD.

IT WAS TRYING TO FIND **ME**, BUT IT FELL THROUGH A PORTAL INTO **POLLY'S WORLD**.

DOORS ARE TRICKY. **WE** LANDED THERE THREE MONTHS IN THE **FUTURE**...

THIS SHIP LANDED FIVE HUNDRED YEARS IN THE **PAST**.

THE SCALE TAILS FOUND HER.

HER?

YEAH.

SHE STARTED MAKING **THINGS** FOR THEM. SILLY THINGS.

THEN THEY WANTED **WEAPONS**.

THEY **HURT** HER IF SHE DIDN'T MAKE THEM.

CRACK ACK

ACK-ACK-ACK-ACK ACK-ACK

CRAAACK

188

189

THE ADVENTURE CONTINUES IN

AVAILABLE NOW!

JUDD WINICK grew up on Long Island, where he spent countless hours doodling, reading **X-Men** comics and the newspaper strip **Bloom County**, and watching **Looney Tunes**. Today Judd lives in San Francisco with his wife, Pam Ling; their two kids; and their cat, Chaka. When Judd isn't collecting far more action figures and vinyl toys than a normal adult, he is a screenwriter and an award-winning cartoonist. Judd has written issues of bestselling comics series, including Batman, Green Lantern, Green Arrow, Justice League, and Star Wars. Judd also appeared as a cast member of MTV's **The Real World: San Francisco** and is the author of the highly acclaimed graphic novel **Pedro and Me**, about his **Real World** castmate and friend, AIDS activist Pedro Zamora. Visit Judd online at **juddspillowfort.com** or on Twitter at **@juddwinick**.